D0897084

WIDE AWAKE

Why can't I sleep?

Julia Akin

ELM HILL

A Division of
HarperCollins Christian Publishing

www.elmhillbooks.com

Wide Awake

Why can't I sleep?

Published in Nashville, Tennessee, by Elm Hill, an imprint of Thomas Nelson. Elm Hill and Thomas Nelson are registered trademarks of HarperCollins Christian Publishing, Inc.

Elm Hill titles may be purchased in bulk for educational, business, fund-raising, or sales promotional use. For information, please e-mail SpecialMarkets@ThomasNelson.com.

Publisher's Note: This novel is a work of fiction. Names, characters, places, and incidents are either products of the author's imagination or used fictitiously. All characters are fictional, and any similarity to people living or dead is purely coincidental.

Library of Congress Cataloging-in-Publication Data

ISBN 978-1-400332441 (Paperback)
ISBN 978-1-400332434 (eBook)

counting those sheep.

Nope. Still wide awake, wide awake, what could be wrong? I think I'd like Mom to sing me a song.

Dad, will you pray?

I sure will, my sweet little pea.

Prayer hands, bow your head and pray with me.

Father in heaven,

I thank you for this day. I thank you for your blessings and for guiding our way. I pray for my child to rest in your love, to know you are with us, and to trust in your Son. Keep us this night, in your tender loving care. May we sleep peacefully knowing you're always there.

Goodnight sweet child.

May God bless you and keep you, all through the night.

Sleep tight.